Published by Scholastic Inc.
90 Old Sherman Turnpike, Danbury, Connecticut 06816.

For information regarding permission, write to:
Disney Licensed Publishing
114 Fifth Avenue, New York, New York 10011.

ISBN 0-7172-6817-9

Designed and produced by Bill SMITH STUDIO.

Printed in the U.S.A.
First printing, April 2004

You Can Do It!

A Story About
Self-Confidence

by **Jacqueline A. Ball**
illustrated by
Duendes del Sur *with*
S.I. International

SCHOLASTIC INC.

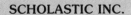

New York   Toronto   London   Auckland   Sydney
Mexico City   New Delhi   Hong Kong   Buenos Aires

Mulan was dreaming that she was swimming in a river. Someone on shore was blowing a whistle. She woke up to find her face wet with rain and Cri-Kee, her lucky cricket, was chirping loudly.

"What's wrong, Cri-Kee?"

With one tiny leg, the cricket pointed outside.

Along with the sounds of rain and thunder, Mulan

heard Khan, her horse, whinnying in fear.

She reached over to the sleeping figure of a

small dragon. "Mushu, wake up!"

"*H*uh? What's up?" the dragon said.

"Khan sounds scared," Mulan said. "I'm afraid he'll break his rope and run away."

"Aw, he'll be all right," said Mushu, yawning. "He's probably just horsing around."

"I need a light to check on him," Mulan insisted.

"Okay, okay," said Mushu. He took a deep breath and blew it out into the night.

But his fire sputtered, then fizzled.

"Huh?" said Mushu. "Any dragon worth his scales has fire stronger than wind and rain!"

"*T*ry again," urged Mulan.

"Stop staring," Mushu complained. "It makes me nervous when you watch."

Mushu drew in another breath and blew it out. But again his fire fizzled.

Khan whinnied louder.

Mulan found her way to Khan in the dark.
She patted him and retied his rope.

Back inside the tent, Mulan found Mushu
slumped in a corner. Clearly, he was upset.

"You're probably just tired," Mulan said kindly.
"Try to get some sleep."

$\mathcal{B}$ut the next morning Mushu was still too upset to even try breathing fire. Mulan wanted to stay and cheer him up, but her group had to take a rope-climbing test. Those who passed would move up to the next level of training.

"Try not to worry," Mulan told him gently.

She rushed over to breakfast, where her friends Chien-Po, Ling, and Yao were waiting.

"Good morning," she greeted them.

"Good morning, Ping," they replied.

No one knew Mulan was really a girl. They thought she was a boy named Ping.

"*I*'m so nervous that I can hardly eat," moaned Chien-Po. "For me, *that's* nervous!"

"I'm nervous, too," said Yao.

"So am I," admitted Mulan. "But we've all worked so hard. We'll be fine."

Ling, their other friend, was silent.

"Are you nervous, Ling?" Mulan asked.

"No," he said. "Not nervous—terrified!"

"You're a great climber!" Mulan protested.

"But I get scared when important people like the captain watch me do something," Ling explained. "I just know I'll fail!"

*J*ust then they heard a gong. So Mulan and her friends hurried outside.

"The rope-climbing test will now begin!" Captain Li Shang yelled. "Ping, you're first."

Mulan scrambled up easily.

The captain pinned a stripe to her uniform. "This means you're promoted to the next level."

"Thank you, sir," said Mulan, beaming.

*T*hen Chien-Po grabbed hold of the rope.
The pole bent under his great weight.

Everyone held their breath. Chien-Po puffed
and strained and finally reached the top.
He slid down and received his stripe.

$\mathcal{Y}$ao took the rope and zipped to the top. "Excellent!" the captain exclaimed. "You've set a new camp record for speed, Yao."

$\mathcal{T}$hen it was Ling's turn.

But as Ling had predicted, he was too nervous with the captain watching. Ling's body shook so hard that he could hardly hold on. When he was halfway up, he lost his grip and slid to the ground.

$\mathcal{M}$ulan held out a hand to help him up.

"I told you," he said sadly.

"I'm sorry, Ling," she said.

"You can take the test again next week, Ling," the captain said. "Until then, you'll be in a different group, with the newest recruits."

The captain left. Chien-Po patted Ling's shoulder. "You'll pass next time," he said.

Ling shook his head. "Maybe not."

That night after dinner, Mulan, Chien-Po, and Yao visited Ling in his tent.

He was still nervous about the test and unhappy with his new group. "They can't seem to learn how to climb the rope," he complained. "Our group leader has tried everything to teach them."

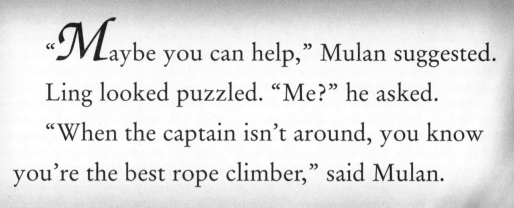

"Maybe you can help," Mulan suggested.
Ling looked puzzled. "Me?" he asked.
"When the captain isn't around, you know
you're the best rope climber," said Mulan.

*L*ater back in Mulan's tent, Mushu wasn't happy, either. Mulan asked him to dry her freshly washed uniform and boil water for her tea—fire-breathing jobs he usually loved. He wouldn't even try, though. He was afraid of failing her again.

"Mushu has lost confidence in himself," she said to Cri-Kee, "just like Ling."

$\mathcal{A}$ few days later, Mulan, Chien-Po, and Yao slipped behind some bamboo to watch Ling work with his group. The young recruits listened carefully to Ling, and they watched intently every time he scampered up the rope.

"*L*ing has confidence in himself with the new recruits," said Mulan.

"Just watch him climb!" Chien-Po said. "If only the captain could see him now!"

Chien-Po's words echoed in Mulan's ears.
"If only the captain could see him now. . . . "
What would a princess do?

"Maybe he can," Mulan suggested. "I think I've got a way!" She rushed off to the captain's tent with a special request.

The day of the test arrived. Ling was pleasantly surprised when all of his old and new friends came to encourage him. "You can do it!" they cheered.

Ling was ready this time. Just as he grabbed the rope, the captain stopped him.

"Ping suggested that I watch you work with the new recruits without your knowledge," the captain said. "And I did. You actually took your test yesterday—you just didn't know it. So you've already passed, with ease."

"Thank you, sir," said Ling firmly, "but I want to take the test again—now."

Ling grabbed the rope. He climbed slowly at first. Then his movements became quicker and more confident. Finally, he scampered to the top.

"Hooray for Ling!" shouted the crowd.

The captain pinned not one but two stripes to Ling's uniform. "Your group leader says you are a fine teacher," Captain Li Shang said. "So from now on, Ling, you'll help him teach rope-climbing to every group of new soldiers."

Ling looked very, very proud.

$\mathcal{M}$ulan hurried to her tent to tell Mushu
and Cri-Kee the good news about Ling. As she
got nearer, she saw something.

"Could it be—smoke?" she wondered.

"Mushu!" she cried. "Your fire is back!"

Mushu shrugged. "Cri-Kee wouldn't eat anything but a toasted rice cake," he said. "I couldn't let our lucky cricket starve."

Cri-Kee winked at Mulan.

Mulan smiled. "May I have one, too?"

"Sure!" Mushu said happily.

That night, Mulan lay in her sleeping bag, reading by the soft glow of Mushu's lowest flame. Cri-Kee, full of rice cakes, was asleep.

Mulan knew that Ling would sleep well tonight, too—now that his self-confidence was back.

"Sometimes, all it takes to get back our confidence is to help others," Mulan thought, sighing happily. "Time to turn out the lights, Mushu. Good night."

The End